HECKELBECK
Gets the Sniffles

By **Wanda Coven**
Illustrated by **Priscilla Burris**

LITTLE SIMON
New York London Toronto Sydney New Delhi

LITTLE SIMON
An imprint of Simon & Schuster Children's Publishing Division
1230 Avenue of the Americas, New York, New York 10020
First Little Simon edition September 2014
Copyright © 2014 by Simon & Schuster, Inc.
All rights reserved, including the right of reproduction in whole or in part in any form.
LITTLE SIMON is a registered trademark of Simon & Schuster, Inc., and associated colophon is a trademark of Simon & Schuster, Inc.
For information about special discounts for bulk purchases, please contact Simon & Schuster Special Sales at 1-866-506-1949 or business@simonandschuster.com.
The Simon & Schuster Speakers Bureau can bring authors to your live event. For more information or to book an event contact the Simon & Schuster Speakers Bureau at 1-866-248-3049 or visit our website at www.simonspeakers.com.
Manufactured in the United States of America 0721 LSC
10 9
Library of Congress Cataloging-in-Publication Data
Coven, Wanda.
Heidi Heckelbeck gets the sniffles / by Wanda Coven ; illustrated by Priscilla Burris. — First edition.
pages cm. — (Heidi Heckelbeck ; 12)
Summary: Heidi is excited about Brewster's Fall Festival, but she catches a cold and her magic may not be enough to make her well in time.
ISBN 978-1-4814-1362-6 (pbk) — ISBN 978-1-4814-1363-3 (hc) —
ISBN 978-1-4814-1364-0 (ebook) [1. Festivals—Fiction. 2. Cold (Disease)—Fiction. 3. Witches—Fiction. 4. Magic—Fiction.] I. Burris, Priscilla, illustrator. II. Title.
PZ7.C83393Hdf 2014
[Fic]—dc23
2013039360

CONTENTS

Chapter 1

SNiFFLES

Ah-choo! sneezed Heidi. *Ah-choo! Ah-choo!*

"Wow, you sure are sneezy today," said Heidi's friend Bruce Bickerson.

Heidi sniffled and smiled. "It's nothing," she said. "Let's finish our leaf pile."

Heidi and Bruce raked the leaves into a colorful mound.

"You go first," Heidi said.

Bruce scurried to the edge of the yard to get a running start. His dog, Frankie, followed close behind.

"One, two, three . . . GO!" shouted Heidi.

Bruce took off, and so did Frankie.
It had become a race! Then, *whump!*
Frankie disappeared into the leaf pile.

"We have a winner!" cried Heidi.

"Hey, that didn't count!" said Bruce.
"Frankie wasn't supposed to race
me."

Heidi covered her mouth to keep from laughing. "Okay, do-over!" she said.

They raked another pile of leaves. Then Bruce put Frankie in his dog run so he wouldn't interfere.

"Ready?" called Heidi.

Bruce got into position and gave the ready signal.

"On your mark!" shouted Heidi. "Get set! GO!"

Bruce ran across the yard and

pounced into the leaves. Then he
shook off the leaves and ran back to
Heidi.

"Your turn!" he said.

Heidi rubbed her forehead.

"What's the matter?" asked Bruce.

"Nothing," Heidi said. "I'm just a little tired."

"Let's get a snack," said Bruce.

"No, thanks," Heidi said, setting down her rake. "I think I'd better get home."

ZONKED

Heidi plopped onto the sofa.

"Dinner's ready," said Mom.

Heidi didn't answer.

"Feel like a taco?" asked Dad.

Heidi loved tacos.

"Nah," she said. "I'm not very hungry."

"Are you sick or something?" asked Henry.

"No-o-o," moaned Heidi.

"Well, you better not be, or you'll miss the Fall Festival," her brother said.

Every year the town of Brewster held a Fall Festival at Thompson's

Homestead. They had scarecrows, pumpkins, a haunted barn, a petting zoo, a hay-bale maze, face-painting, bounce houses, hayrides, and lots of carnival games with prizes. Heidi especially liked the haunted barn. This year Heidi and her best friend, Lucy Lancaster, planned to go through the haunted barn together.

"I'm FINE," Heidi said.

Then she felt a tickle in her nose.

Ah-choo! she sneezed. *Ah-choo!* *Ah-choo!*

"Uh-oh," Henry said.

"What?" said Heidi.

"You don't sound very good."

"I just need some orange juice," Heidi said, sitting up.

Heidi forced down a glass of orange juice, but it didn't make her feel any better. Then she made an Aunt Trudy Special: half a cup of honey and half a cup of apple cider vinegar. It smelled awful. But there was no way she was going to miss the Fall Festival. She plugged her nose and drank it down.

"Yuck," she said.

"How about some chicken soup?"
Dad suggested.

"Maybe later," said Heidi.

"How about a good night's rest?"
Mom said. "Maybe you'll feel better
in the morning."

Rest sounded unexpectedly good.
Heidi dragged herself off the couch
and plodded upstairs. Mom helped

her into her favorite blue polka-dot pajamas. Then Heidi crawled right into bed.

And *zonk*, she was out.

GROUCHY

I feel horrible, thought Heidi when she woke up. Her throat hurt and her head was stuffed up. She pulled the covers over her face and groaned. Then she yanked the covers right back down. *No!* she told herself. *I have to get up! Today I'm going to help Aunt Trudy set up her booth for the Fall Festival.* Heidi slid out from under the warm covers and plunked her feet on the floor. She rubbed her eyes with the backs of her fists and snuffed up the gook in her nose.

Then she shuffled to the bathroom, splashed cold water on her face, and looked in the mirror.

"You can do this," Heidi said to herself.

She straggled to her bedroom and

sluggishly put on her jeans, a white daisy T-shirt, and a lavender hoodie. She brushed her hair, and headed to the kitchen.

"Well, if it isn't our late sleeper!" said Dad cheerily as he looked up from his bowl of granola.

Heidi sniffled and forced a smile.

Mom closed the lid on the waffle iron

and walked over to Heidi. She put her
hand on Heidi's forehead.

"You're warm," Mom said.

"I'm warm because I just got out of bed," said Heidi as she landed on her chair with a thud.

Mom frowned.

"Ahoy, matey!" shouted Henry, who was sitting in the chair beside her. He was wearing a fake handlebar mustache.

Heidi covered her ears.

Henry shoveled a handful of a waffle into his mouth. Part of his mustache went in with it.

"Want some grub?" asked Henry as he pulled the mustache out of his mouth.

Heidi didn't answer.

Henry picked up his plastic sword
and poked his sister in the side.

"Ow!" cried Heidi, yanking the
sword from Henry's hand. "Quit it!"

"Well, ex-CUSE me!" said Henry.

Mom placed a waffle and a cup of tea in front of Heidi.

"Mom, Heidi's in a bad mood," Henry said.

"Heidi doesn't feel too well," said Mom.

"I feel FINE," Heidi said.

"You're a grouch," said Henry.

"Leave me alone!" yelled Heidi.

Henry picked up his plate and walked to the sink.

Dad got up and kneeled behind Heidi.

"Maybe you should go back to bed, pump-kin," he suggested.

"No," said Heidi. "I promised Aunt Trudy

I'd help set up her booth for the Fall Festival."

"Aunt Trudy will understand if you don't feel well," said Mom.

Heidi sighed. "But I DO feel well," she lied.

She took a sip of tea and ate a bite of waffle. "See?" she said. "I have a normal appetite and everything!"

Mom and Dad gave each other a worried look.

"I'm good!" Heidi said. "Watch—I'll prove it!"

She jumped up from the table and began to do jumping jacks. She did ten in a row and stopped. Her head throbbed, but she acted like she was okay. "How's that?"

"Not bad," Dad said.

Mom didn't seem so sure, but she went along with it. "Okay, we'll let you help Aunt Trudy," she said. "But if you're not feeling any better, I'm going to bring you straight home."

"I feel GREAT!" said Heidi. Then she ran upstairs to change.

Chapter 4

GERMS!

Heidi and Mom met Aunt Trudy in front of a white canopy tent. Under the tent stood three banquet tables, a bunch of folding chairs, and several boxes of Aunt Trudy's homemade perfumes. She also had two large boxes full of fall decorations and a wheelbarrow filled with pumpkins.

"Let's get started!" said Aunt Trudy as she pulled out three chocolate-brown tablecloths.

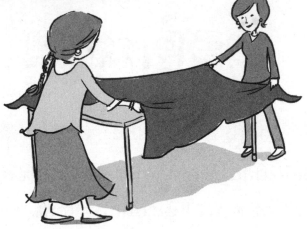

Mom and Aunt Trudy unfolded the tablecloths and spread them over all the tables. Heidi rummaged through the decorations and pulled out two scarecrows, a bag full of

colored leaves, and
a stuffed witch
with black-and-
white-striped
stockings. She
hung the scare-
crows on the tent's poles in front of
the booth. Then she set the stuffed
witch on the center table and scat-
tered some of the fall leaves across

the tablecloths. After that she helped her aunt arrange the perfumes on the tables.

Aunt Trudy made perfumes in all kinds of fragrances, like jasmine, cherry blossom, vanilla brown sugar, and peony. She also had some fall fragrances, like pumpkin spice and caramel apple. Heidi liked lily of the valley the best. She squirted some on her wrist and sniffed. She couldn't smell a thing. *Ugh*, she thought. *My nose is too clogged.*

Then Heidi noticed
Melanie Maplethorpe
standing in front of
Aunt Trudy's booth.
Melanie had a tray
of cider doughnuts
in her hands.

"Well, well," said
Melanie. "Now I know
why it's so STINKY
around here!" Then she
took one hand off the tray
and pinched her nose. "And it's NOT
the perfume!"

Heidi tried to ignore Melanie, but

she couldn't. Heidi felt mad *and* sick.
She opened her mouth to say something, and then she felt a tingle in
her nose.

AH-CHOO! sneezed Heidi.

Melanie looked at her doughnuts.

"EWWW!" she shouted. "You got GERMS all over my doughnuts!"

"I didn't mean to!" cried Heidi.

"Ugh! That is just SO disgusting!" yelled Melanie.

Heidi's mom ran to the rescue.

"Settle down, girls!" she said. "I'll pay for the doughnuts."

Mom got her wallet and handed Melanie twenty dollars.

"We're so sorry about your dough-nuts," said Mom. "Heidi has a cold."

Melanie put the money in her jacket pocket and stormed off. She shoved the doughnuts—tray and all—into a trash can. Then she ran back to her booth, where she and her dad were selling doughnuts and muffins.

Mom hugged Heidi. "Don't worry about Smell-a-nie," Mom said. "She'll get over it."

"I doubt it," said Heidi. Then she looked at her mother. "Did you just say SMELL-A-NIE?"

Mom smiled. "You bet I did."

GROUNDED

Heidi lifted a pumpkin from the wheelbarrow and lugged it to the front of the booth. She propped the pumpkin in front of one of the scarecrows. Then she put her hand to her head. *Wow, I feel so tired,* she thought. She sniffled and sat on one of the folding chairs.

"How are you feel-ing?" asked Mom.

"I just need a little rest," Heidi said.

Mom walked over and felt Heidi's head.

"You're very warm," said Mom. "I'm afraid I'm going to have to take you home."

Aunt Trudy nodded in agreement.

"No-o-o-o!" begged Heidi. "I'll be okay."

"Try to take a little nap," suggested Aunt Trudy, "and come back this afternoon."

Heidi thought about it for a moment. Maybe a nap would do the trick.

"Okay," she said. "But I'm coming right back."

"Good," Aunt Trudy said. "I'll be waiting."

Aunt Trudy gave Heidi a great big hug. Then Heidi and Mom walked to the car. Heidi felt like she was walking in outer space. She flopped onto the backseat and shut her eyes.

The next thing Heidi knew, they were in their driveway. Mom helped Heidi get to her room. She tucked Heidi into bed and kissed her on the forehead.

"Don't forget to wake me up for the festival," mumbled Heidi.

✦ ✦ ✳ ◎ ✦

Heidi woke up three hours later. She felt awful, but she rolled out of bed and made her way downstairs to the kitchen. Dad and Henry had their jackets on.

"Where are you going?" asked Heidi in a raspy voice that didn't sound at all like her own.

"They're going to the festival," said Mom. "I called Lucy and told her you wouldn't be able to make it."

Heidi covered her face and began to cry.

"It's okay," Mom said, wrapping her arms around Heidi. "We'll have lots of fun right here. We can make cinnamon spice tea and watch your favorite movie, *The Witch Switch*."

"I'll bring you a treat," promised Henry.

"And I'll try to win a stuffed animal for you," added Dad.

Then they slipped out the back door.

Heidi buried her face in Mom's sweater. She cried until her nose became so stuffy that she couldn't breathe through it. Then she looked at her mom and said, "Why does everything bad happen to me?"

Chapter 6

QUiCK FiX

If only I could get rid of this stupid cold, thought Heidi, *then I could go to the festival.* She flopped onto her bed. *It could take days to get better, and by then the festival will be long gone.* Heidi threw her stuffed owl against the wall. It bounced off and rolled

under her dust ruffle. She reached over to pick it up and noticed her *Book of Spells* under the bed. *Wait a second,* she thought. *Maybe I CAN get better faster.* She pulled the book out from under the bed.

"There has to be a spell to cure a cold," she said to herself.

Heidi looked at the Contents page and found a whole chapter on health. There were remedies for everything from rashes to back pain. Then she found a spell called "No More Sickness!"

"Bingo!" said Heidi as she began to read the spell.

No More Sickness!

Do you have an upset stomach? Are you the kind of witch who has a tendency to get tonsillitis? Or perhaps you've just come down with a rotten cold. If anything ails you, then this is the spell for you!

Ingredients:
1 teaspoon of cinnamon
1 cup of peppermint tea
2 tablespoons of ketchup

Mix the ingredients together in a mug. Hold your Witches of Westwick medallion in one hand. Place your other hand over the mix and chant the following words:

SNIFFLE-DEE-DOO!

SNIFFLE-DEE-DAY!

MAKE THIS SICKNESS GO AWAY!

Drink the potion and feel your sickness disappear!

The thought of drinking that mixture of ingredients was totally disgusting, but it wasn't as bad as feeling sick. Heidi bookmarked the page. Then she slid into her fuzzy blue bunny slippers and headed downstairs. She paused on the bottom stair and listened. Mom was on the phone. Heidi tiptoed past her office and into the kitchen.

She plopped a tea bag into a mug and filled the mug with warm water. Then Heidi added the cinnamon

and ketchup and stirred
the ingredients together.
When she was done,
she shuffled toward the
stairs with her potion.

"Is that you, Heidi?"
called Mom.

Heidi froze and held her mug close. "Yup, it's me," she said. "I, uh, just wanted some juice."

"Good," said Mom. "Are you up for a movie?"

"I would much rather go to the festival," Heidi said.

"I know, but not this time," Mom said apologetically. "I'll get some pillows and blankets."

Heidi went to her room and shut the door. She sat on the floor and placed her Witches of Westwick medallion around her neck. She held

the medallion in one hand and put her other hand over the mug. Then she chanted the spell. For a moment the mixture bubbled, then it became still again. Heidi took a sip. *It's a good thing I'm too sick to taste this,* she thought. Then she guzzled it down.

Chapter 7

RiBBiT!

Heidi set down the mug and breathed through her nose. The air went right in—just like it was supposed to. *No sniffles!* she thought. Then she swallowed. *No sore throat!* Heidi hopped to her feet and jumped up and down. *I don't have a single ache or pain!* She did a little happy dance. *I feel all better!* she thought. *Now I can go to the festival!*

Heidi couldn't wait to tell her mother. She ran from her room and called to her mom from the top of the stairs.

"RIBBIT!" she shouted. "RIBBIT! RIBBIT!"

Heidi covered her mouth with her hand. *Oh no!* she thought. *I sound just like a frog! Something must've gone wrong!*

Heidi thundered downstairs and ran straight into Mom's office. Mom twirled her chair around.

"What in the world is going on?" asked Mom. "You sounded like a herd of buffalo on the stairs. Are you feeling better?"

Heidi pointed frantically to her mouth.

Mom looked puzzled. Heidi opened her mouth and pointed down her throat.

"You're so silly," she said. "Just tell
me if your throat still hurts."

Heidi shook her head and bugged
out her eyes. She grabbed a pen from

Mom's pencil cup. Then she peeled
off a sticky note and wrote Mom a
message:

I used a spell
to get rid of my
cold and something
went wrong! Now I
have a frog in my
throat! Help!

Mom read the note and looked at
Heidi. "Are you sure?" she asked.

Heidi nodded.

"Try to say something," said Mom.

"RIBBIT!" said Heidi.

"Oh dear!" said Mom.

"RIBBIT! RIBBIT! RIBBIT!" Heidi
said, which translated to "Please help
me!"

Mom put her hands to her cheeks.
"Oh, Heidi!" she said. "You've done it
AGAIN!"

Chapter 8

SAY SOMETHING!

Heidi began to cry again.

She peeled off another sticky note and wrote:

Do you think Aunt Trudy can help me?

"She's still at the festival," said Mom. "But don't forget I'm a witch too. Maybe I can figure out what went wrong. Show me the spell you used."

Mom rarely used her witching skills. She tried to live as normal a life as anyone. But today she had to make an exception.

Heidi jotted down another note:

I'll get my book. Be right back!

Heidi ran and got her *Book of Spells*. Then she opened it to the "No More Sickness!" spell. Mom studied the ingredients.

"Hmm," she said. "What kind of tea did you use?"

Heidi answered on a sticky note.

Mint.

"Let's go to the kitchen and have a look," said Mom.

Heidi raced to the kitchen, pulled the tea from the cupboard, and handed it to Mom.

Mom opened the box. She sniffed the tea bags. Then she looked at the label. "Interesting," she said.

"Ribbit?" questioned Heidi, which really meant "What?" in frog.

Mom pointed to

the picture on the box. "You used
spearmint tea. The recipe calls for
peppermint."

Heidi looked puzzled.

"They're different," said Mom.
"Spearmint and peppermint are different enough to affect your spell."

Heidi hung her head.

"Now, hold on," said Mom, "and I'll see what I can do."

Mom scurried to her office and came back with her Witches of Westwick medallion. Then she pulled a container of salt and a jar of honey from the cupboard. Heidi sat on a kitchen stool and watched her mom squeeze half a cup of honey into a bowl. Then she added a teaspoon of salt and mixed them together. Mom spread the mix on Heidi's neck  with her fingertips. Then she picked up her medallion and chanted a spell.

Sha-zing, sha-zang, sha-zog.
Remove this croaking frog!

Heidi sat and stared at Mom.

"Don't just sit there," said Mom.

"Please say something!"

Heidi tried to think of something clever to say. Then she opened her mouth and went, "OINK! OINK!"

Mom clonked the palm of her hand on her forehead. "Oh no!" she cried. "Now you sound like a pig!"

Heidi smiled. "Just kidding!" she said.

"Not funny!" said Mom.

"Sorry," Heidi said.

"That's all I could think of to say."

Mom ruffled Heidi's hair.

But there was still one problem.

TWO WORDS

Ah-choo! sneezed Heidi. *Ah-choo! Ah-choo!*

She felt completely yucky all over again.

"Sorry, no more fix-it spells," said Mom. "Health cures are too risky. You're just going to have to get well the old-fashioned way."

"Ugh," said Heidi.

"Come on," said Mom. "Let's wash off this honey mixture. Then we can make a nest and watch *The Witch Switch*."

After washing off the sticky mixture, Heidi and Mom snuggled on the

couch and watched the movie. It was dark when Henry and Dad got home. The boys sat on the couch and tried to cheer Heidi up.

"I brought you a bag of kettle corn AND a frosted pumpkin sugar cookie," said Henry.

"Thanks," said Heidi—even though she didn't feel like eating anything.

"I got you something too," Dad said.

He pulled a stuffed black cat from behind his back and handed it to Heidi. The cat had an arched back, a frizzed tail, green eyes, and red stitching on its nose and mouth.

"I won it in the football toss," Dad said proudly.

"He had to toss a LOT of footballs,"

Henry whispered.

"I love it," said Heidi, admiring the cat. "What else did you guys do?"

"We went on the hayride," said Henry. "But it was really bumpy. Then we went in the maze."

"And Henry got lost," Dad said.

"I just got a little mixed up," said Henry.

"Did you go in the haunted barn?" asked Heidi.

"Believe it or not, I did!" Henry said.

Henry had never been in the haunted barn before.

"How was it?" asked Heidi.

"Really, really scary," said Henry. "But I loved it!"

Heidi looked at the floor. "I sure wish I could've gone," she said miserably. "The haunted barn is my favorite thing ever. Now I have to wait a WHOLE year until the next one."

Heidi slumped on the sofa and put a pillow over her face.

"Two words," said Henry. "That STINKS."

Chapter 10

A SURPRISE

Heidi missed a whole week of school. By Saturday she felt like her old self.

"Guess what?" said Henry at breakfast.

"What?" asked Heidi.

"Today you're going to get a big surprise!"

"Why?" Heidi asked.

"Because you missed the Fall Festival," said Mom.

"What kind of a surprise?" asked Heidi.

"A haunted house!" said Henry.

Heidi squealed. "I LOVE haunted houses!" she said. "Where is it?"

"In the garage," said Dad.

The Heckelbecks had a big garage. It even had wooden stairs that led to an upstairs storage area.

"It has a real ghost and every-thing!" said Henry.

"But you have to wait until dark," Mom said.

"Can Lucy come?" asked Heidi.

Mom and Dad looked at each other.

"Lucy had other plans today," said Mom.

"Rats," said Heidi.

"But I still can't wait!"

Heidi and Henry spent the day at Aunt Trudy's. They carved jack-o'-lanterns and made cupcakes with monster faces. After supper Heidi had to wait in her room until her family was ready. At six o'clock her bedroom door creaked open. A hand reached in and turned off the light. Then she saw Aunt Trudy in the doorway. She had on a jet-black dress with a jagged hem. Her hair had been teased, and she wore smoky eye makeup and bright red lipstick. She held a glowing candelabra in one hand.

"Hello, Heidi," she said in a deeper voice than usual. "My name is Raven, and I'm going to take you to the *haunted* house."

Heidi jumped up and followed

Raven outside and around to the garage. The jack-o'-lanterns had been lit and displayed around the outside. Strands of twinkly orange lights hung from the garage and covered the bushes. A sign on a stake in front of

the garage said FOR SALE, and under-neath it said DIRT CHEAP.

Raven shook her head sadly.

"I've tried to sell this house for fifty years, but no one wants to buy it."

"How come?" asked Heidi.

"Are you sure you want to know?" Raven asked.

"Positive," said Heidi.

Raven glanced at the upstairs window of the garage as if she were checking for something. Then she

looked back at Heidi. "This house is haunted," she whispered.

Heidi's eyes grew wide. Even though she knew there were no such things as ghosts, she began to feel a tingle in her spine.

"By what?" questioned Heidi.

"By a *ghost*," Raven whispered.

Raven opened the door to the garage, and a cold, eerie mist swept over Heidi.

They stepped inside, and Raven went on whispering. "No one ever knows when the ghost will appear," she said as she looked uncertainly all around her.

Heidi heard a door creak somewhere in the garage. The inside of the garage had been made to look like rooms in somebody's house.

"Do you think the ghost will come out today?" asked Heidi.

Raven paused for a moment. "We shall soon see," she whispered.

Then Heidi heard someone moan.

"I WANT TO COME DOWN!" said an eerie voice from up the wooden stairs.

"What was that?" asked Heidi, biting the corner of a fingernail.

Raven looked up. "Oh no," she whispered. "I fear it may be the *ghost*!"

A dusty piano then began to play

"Chopsticks" all by itself. Heidi never realized how creepy "Chopsticks" could sound in a dark, spooky garage.

She pointed at the piano. "How is it doing that?"

"The ghost likes to play the piano," said Raven. "But it's funny, it doesn't seem to need to be at the piano to play it."

Then the voice from upstairs

wailed again. "I WANT TO COME
DOWN!" it cried.

"Come," Raven said. "I'd like to
show you the dining room."

Heidi followed Raven into the dining room.

The table was set for dinner. A
mummy sat at one end of the table

and a skeleton at the other. A zombie boy sat on one side.

"I'm hungry!" said the zombie boy. "Would you please take the lid off my dinner?"

Raven nodded to Heidi.

Heidi looked at the domed plat-ter. *Don't be afraid,* she told herself.

Remember, this is all fake. Then she bit her bottom lip, lifted the lid, and screamed.

"*Aaaaaaaaaah!*"

There was a head on the platter, and it waggled its tongue at Heidi! Heidi grabbed on to Raven and held tight.

"Yuck!" complained the zombie

boy. "We had somebody's head for dinner LAST night!"

Heidi took a closer look at the ghoulish head on the platter. It looked an awful lot like Dad.

Then a door banged upstairs.

"I'M COMING DOWN!" said the ghostly voice.

Chapter 11

BOO!

Raven led Heidi into the living room. Huge spiders hung from the ceiling. An old lady rocked in a chair with her knitting. A black cat sat beside her. It hissed at Heidi. Then the coffin coffee table in front of the old lady began to creak. The lid slowly opened, and a

vampire boy rose from inside.

"Good evening . . . ," he said. "I vant to suck your blood!"

Heidi hid behind Raven.

"Oh, don't mind him," said the old lady. "He just wants his bottle."

The old lady handed Heidi a baby
bottle full of what looked like blood.

Heidi shut her eyes and handed the
bottle to the vampire boy. He slurped
it down.

"Thank you," said the vampire boy. "That vuz vunderful!"

Then the boy lay back down in the coffin and shut the lid.

"I'M COMING DOWN!" said the spooky voice from upstairs.

The old lady stopped knitting and looked at Heidi.

"Little girl, you must get out of this house!" she warned. "Get out while you can!"

The wailing voice got a little bit louder. "I'M COMING DOWN!"

The dim lights began to flicker.

"We'd better go," urged Raven. She rushed Heidi toward the door.

But it was too late! They ran right

into the ghost on the bottom stair.
The ghost wore a ragged dress and
had a sheet over its face. It hopped
from the stair and landed in front of
Heidi.

"Boo!" said the ghost.

Heidi screamed and ran out the
door and onto the driveway.

"WAIT!" shouted the ghost as she chased Heidi out of the garage. "It's ME, LUCY!"

Heidi turned around. "Lucy? Is that really YOU?"

"Yes!" cried Lucy.

Then everyone came out: Mom, Dad, Henry the zombie, Aunt Trudy,

and the vampire boy, who was really Heidi's friend Bruce.

Heidi began to laugh.

"Did we scare you?" asked Henry.

"Did you EVER!" said Heidi, still catching her breath. "That haunted house was the BEST!"

"Yes!" said Henry, pumping his fist.

Everyone cheered. Then they all went into the Heckelbecks' house and had monster cupcakes and goblets filled with blood . . . which, of course, was really just fruit punch.

"What's the matter, Lucy?" asked Heidi.

"Nothing," her friend said coldly.

Heidi looked at Bruce to see if he knew anything. Bruce looked at the ground.

Heidi turned back to Lucy. "What's going on?" she pressed.

Lucy lowered her eyebrows and

An excerpt from *Heidi Heckelbeck Is Not a Thief!*

pushed her lips together. "As if you didn't know," she said.

"What are you talking about?" asked Heidi.

"Okay, I'll tell you," Lucy said crossly. "My lollipop pen is missing! It wasn't in my backpack when I got home last night."

Heidi blinked in disbelief.

"So please give it BACK, right now!" Lucy said firmly.

"But I don't have it," said Heidi. "Maybe it fell out of your backpack at Bruce's."

"I checked all over," Bruce said.

An excerpt from *Heidi Heckelbeck Is Not a Thief!*

"Maybe it's in my dad's car," Heidi suggested.

"Nice try," Lucy said.

"What's THAT supposed to mean?" asked Heidi.

"Think about it," said Lucy. "You wanted a lollipop pen, then your aunt didn't get you the right one—and now mine is MISSING!"

Heidi's face fell. "You really think I stole your pen?" she asked.

Lucy looked away for a moment. "Well, it sure looks that way."

"Wow," said Heidi. "What kind of friend do you think I am?"

An excerpt from *Heidi Heckelbeck Is Not a Thief!*